Other Books by
R.L. STINE

THE ADVENTURES OF SHRINKMAN

Text copyright © 2000 Parachute Press
Cover illustration by Tim Jacobus

A Parachute Press Book

Published by Amazon Publishing
P.O. Box 400818
Las Vegas, NV 89140

ISBN-13: 9781612183282
ISBN-10: 161218328X

R.L. STINE

THE ADVENTURES OF SHRINKMAN

amazon publishing

INTRODUCTION

• R.L. STINE •

People always ask me where I get my ideas. Most of the time I don't know how to answer that question. But I know where I got the idea for *The Adventures of Shrinkman*. I stole it—from myself.

When my brother Bill and I were kids, our parents measured our height every month. We stood as tall as we could with our backs to the wall. They used a yardstick and made a pencil mark at the top of our heads.

Sometimes I tried to cheat by standing on tiptoe. But they always caught me. I don't know why

Bill and I thought this was so much fun. But we really enjoyed seeing the pencil marks go up the wall as we grew taller.

One day when I was ten or eleven, my mom stared at the pencil mark she had just made. Her eyes went wide. "I don't believe it. You're an inch shorter."

I gasped. "Huh?"

Bill laughed. "You shrunk!" he cried.

"Let me see it," I said. I spun around to examine the mark on the wall.

Then Bill and Mom burst out laughing. They were playing a joke on me.

I didn't think it was funny. I began to think: *What if I DID begin to shrink?*

At age ten, I was already writing stories. I went to my room, sat down in front of my big black type-writer, and started to write a story about a shrink-ing boy. I wrote it like a comic book with drawings and thought balloons.

I loved to read comic books when I was a kid. And I tried to draw my own. Then I'd show them to my friends. I remember my friends really liked the one I wrote about kids who shrink down to the size of insects.

I also remember that Bill and I weren't the only kids who liked to measure our height. Most kids thought a lot about whether they were going to be short or tall. Most kids want to be about the *same* as everyone else in their class. They don't want to stand out by being taller or shorter than everyone else.

I think this is one reason why stories about giants and little people have been popular for many, many years.

I remember one movie that came out when I was a teenager that captured all my fears about shrinking. It was called *The Incredible Shrinking Man*.

In this film, a man is sunning himself on a boat when a strange mist floats over him. He is sprinkled with glitter. Later he is sprayed by bug spray while driving his car. And soon after that, he starts to shrink.

To his horror, he gets smaller and smaller. When he is three feet tall, the whole nation becomes interested in him. When he reaches six inches tall, he's forced to live in a dollhouse. But he isn't safe there. The family cat has its eyes on him. The cat is hungrily determined to break in and grab him.

That was really scary.

The next year, Hollywood brought out a movie that was an answer to *The Incredible Shrinking Man*. This film was called *Attack of the 50 Foot Woman*.

In this film, a woman drives through an enormous radioactive bubble and starts to grow. Soon she is fifty feet tall—big enough to frighten the whole town and get revenge against her no-good husband. To tell you the truth, it wasn't that scary, but it was pretty funny.

My all-time favorite shrinking movie is *Honey, I Shrunk the Kids*. The nutty scientist father accidentally shrinks his two kids and two kids next door down to the size of insects.

He doesn't see them. He sweeps them up and dumps them in the trash. Now the tiny kids battle horrible danger as they try to make their way through the jungle of grass, across the backyard, and back to their house.

The film is hilarious and terrifying at the same time, which is why I like it so much.

After seeing so many movies and TV shows about people shrinking or growing into giants, I decided to write my own. That's why I came up with *The Adventures of Shrinkman*.

I remembered how much I liked to draw comics in fifth grade. So I made Danny a comic book artist. He draws comics about a popular movie superhero named Shrinkman. But it all becomes too real for Danny when *he* actually begins to shrink.

Why is this happening to him? He hasn't a clue. But he has an even more terrifying question: Is he going to shrink smaller and smaller until he disappears *forever*?

RL Stine

CHAPTER 1

Megan Burleigh turned away from her beakers and test tubes and squinted her dark brown eyes at me. She frowned and the dimples in her round cheeks grew deeper.

"What are you doing, Danny?" she asked. "Drawing another comic strip about that shrinking guy?"

I leaned over the lab table, penciling in a long flowing cape. "His name is Shrinkman," I said, sighing. "Not That Shrinking Guy."

Megan calls him that just to be annoying. She knows I'm obsessed with two things—basketball and Shrinkman. She knows that I draw Shrinkman comics whenever I have a spare moment.

And she hates it.

Megan doesn't like it that I can do something she can't do. Megan is the most competitive person I've ever met. She likes to win. She likes to be the best at everything.

"What is the point of being a loser?" she says.

My name is Danny Marin, and I'm not a loser. I'm just different from most fifth graders.

When I'm not out practicing my slam dunk, I like to stay in my room for hours drawing Shrinkman comics. If I go slow and concentrate, I can draw Shrinkman almost as well as Duke Barnes. Duke is the artist who created him.

I go to all the Shrinkman movies, too. I guess my favorite is *Shrinkman vs. Mister Big*. I also loved the special effects in *A Little Surprise for Shrinkman*, although the ending was dumb.

I mean, you can't keep Shrinkman in a jelly jar. He'd get big again and break the glass.

I wrote a letter to Duke Barnes about that, but he didn't answer me.

My parents say I can go to art school this summer. I'm only eleven now. But if I keep practicing, maybe I'll get good enough by the time I'm twenty or so to take over the comic strip. Or at least help Duke Barnes with it.

That would be so cool.

"Danny, we're supposed to be working on our Science Fair projects," Megan said. She held a test tube up to the light and studied it. It was half-filled with a purple liquid.

"I *am* working on my project," I replied, filling in Shrinkman's cape. "But I don't see the point, Megan. Everyone knows you're going to win the competition and walk home with the thousand-dollar prize."

"Of course I am." She brushed her honey-blond hair off the shoulders of her blue tank top. "I really really *really* desperately want to win that money."

She poured the purple liquid into the lab sink. It made a fizzy sound as it disappeared down the drain.

"You can't draw a comic for a science project," she said. "Mr. Clarkus definitely won't allow it."

Mr. Clarkus is the science teacher at Baker Elementary School. He looks like a big, sloppy whale. His blubber belly is always hanging out from his shirt.

He doesn't like me. I think it's because he overheard me calling him Clarkus the Carcass.

Everyone calls him that. But *I'm* the one he overheard saying it. I've been getting C-minuses in science ever since.

Megan was pouring a clear liquid into a boiling, bubbling blue liquid. "What's your project?" I asked her, sniffing hard. It smelled kind of sour.

Her dark eyes flashed. She made a zipping motion over her lips. "I can't tell."

"Excuse me? What do you *mean* you can't tell?"

"It's a secret mixture that will amaze the world. If I tell you what it is, it will spoil the surprise."

I laughed. "You don't know *what* you're doing, do you?"

The liquid fizzed over the glass beaker. A grin spread over her face. "Of *course* I know what I'm doing; I told you, my great-great-grandmother was a witch."

I rolled my eyes. "Yeah, sure."

She sneered at me. "At least I'm not trying to pass off a comic strip as a science project."

I held the drawings up to show her. "It's very scientific. See? Shrinkman makes himself tiny enough to enter a human brain. Then, as he travels through each part of the brain, I explain how it works and what it does."

Megan shook her head. "It's totally lame."

"It's a good project," I insisted. "I described it to Clarkus the Carcass, and he said—"

Uh-oh.

First I saw the wide shadow roll over me. Then I saw Mr. Clarkus standing beside the lab table.

Frowning. His eyes cold. His teeth gritted tightly.

He *heard!*

I gasped—and swallowed my gum.

It stuck in the back of my throat. I started to choke. Megan slapped me hard on the back. But the gum didn't move.

I wheezed, choking, struggling to suck in air.

Megan handed me a glass of water off the table. I tilted it to my lips, and drank it down.

There. Finally. The gum went down. I could breathe.

I sucked in several deep breaths, waiting for my heart to stop racing.

"Danny, are you okay?" Mr. Clarkus asked, studying me with his cold, marble blue eyes.

"Yeah. Fine."

"Then come with me," he said, motioning to the lab door with his pale, blubbery hand. "I think you and I need to have a talk."

CHAPTER 2

"What did Mr. Clarkus want to talk to you about?" Megan asked.

I groaned. "I don't want to talk about it."

It was the next afternoon, a Saturday, and Megan and I were walking to the Baker Cineplex to see the new Shrinkman movie—*Shrinkman's Biggest Adventure.*

I'd already seen it twice. But I wanted Megan to see it.

My dad is the projectionist at the Baker Cineplex. That means he shows the films in all eight theaters.

It's a pretty hard job. He has to keep moving from theater to theater to make sure the film is in focus and everything is running right.

You'd think they'd let me into the movies for free since Dad works there. But I have to pay like everyone else.

We crossed Mill Street, and the theater came into view on the next corner. A few kids sat on the curb outside the ticket office. But there wasn't a long line.

The Shrinkman movies aren't really very popular. I don't know anyone besides me who goes to see them three or four times. A lot of kids say that a superhero who can shrink down to the size of a bug is dumb. He gets so small you can barely see him.

That's because the special-effects budgets on the movies aren't very high. They don't have much money to make it look real.

You need a good imagination to appreciate Shrinkman movies.

As we made our way to the theater, Megan poked me playfully in the ribs. "So? What did he say to you?"

I stopped. "You mean Carcass? He told me that nicknames can be cruel. That I should call people by their real names."

Megan's eyes burned into mine. "And what else?"

I sighed. "He said my science project was lame. He said I had to think up a better one."

I hated the I-told-you-so smile on Megan's face. She is a good friend, but sometimes I'd like to punch her really hard.

"He said if I don't shape up and start getting better grades, he's going to tell Coach Gray to cut me from the basketball team."

Thinking about it made me angry. I stepped away from her. "Do we have to talk about this?" I said. "I don't really want to think about Carcass now. Can't we just enjoy the movie?"

She shrugged. "No problem."

We bought tickets and made our way inside. Megan bought a huge bucket of popcorn. She's so competitive, she always has to have the *biggest* popcorn bucket they sell. She also bought an enormous bag of Twizzlers.

I wasn't feeling hungry—but I stopped when I saw a vending machine, almost hidden in the dark shadows against the wall.

I stepped up to it, and my eyes scanned the blue lettering against the black surface of the machine. Shrinkman Cola.

"Cool!" I exclaimed.

I bent down and gazed into the little window on the front of the machine. Behind the glass, I could see a blue and black bottle with the familiar Shrinkman logo. Shrinkman Cola.

I had to try it.

I pulled a dollar from my wallet and slid it into the chrome slot.

The machine clinked and clunked. And a bottle rolled out at the bottom.

Megan rolled her eyes. "I can't believe you bought that, Danny. Will you buy *anything* with the word Shrinkman on it?"

"Probably," I replied.

I twisted off the top of the Shrinkman Cola bottle. The dark liquid fizzed up to the rim of the opening.

Before it spilled over, I raised it to my mouth and took several long swallows.

"Yuck—!"

I wanted to spit.

"This tastes *gross!*" I cried. I groaned and made a disgusted face. "It's kind of bitter. It—it tastes totally weird!"

Megan laughed. "Maybe that's why they hid the drink machine way back here in the corner."

I kept swallowing, trying to get the horrible taste from my mouth. "What was Duke Barnes *thinking*?" I cried. I tossed the half-full bottle into a trash basket. "Yuck."

We went into the theater and took seats in the third row. I chewed up four of Megan's Twizzlers, but it didn't help get rid of the rotten Shrinkman Cola taste.

I turned to the back and searched for my dad in the projection booth. The lights were on back there, but I couldn't see him.

The theater lights dimmed. The Coming Attractions flashed onto the screen. I'd seen them all before. I wished I could fast-forward through them and get to the movie.

When *Shrinkman's Biggest Adventure* finally started and Shrinkman flew across the screen in his dazzling blue cape, I raised my feet to the seat in front of me and settled back to enjoy the film.

"His cape is one-size-fits-all," Megan whispered.

Ha ha. Did she have any idea how lame her Shrinkman jokes were?

I grabbed a big handful of popcorn from her bucket and stared straight ahead at the screen.

The movie was even better the third time.

The big scene where Shrinkman hides in the gangster boss's shirt pocket was totally awesome. And when Shrinkman shrinks to the size of a watermelon seed and starts climbing up the gangster's nose, everyone in the theater cheered and screamed.

Everyone except Megan, that is.

"You didn't think it was awesome?" I asked, walking up the aisle as the closing credits ran.

She shrugged. "It was okay. But it's all a little hard to believe."

We stopped at the steps that led up to the projection room. Megan's dark eyes studied me. I could see she was thinking hard.

"Danny, don't you think Shrinkman is kind of a waste of time?"

I blinked. "What do you mean?"

"Well…you could be out practicing basketball," she replied. "The team is really counting on you…"

"What does Shrinkman have to do with basketball?" I asked. "I practice for basketball all the time. But Shrinkman is a lot more important. He's—"

"But if you got serious about basketball and really worked hard, the Tigers could win the city championship this year!" Megan declared.

I shook my head. "There's more to life than *winning*," I said. "Is that *all* you think about? Just winning, winning, winning?"

"Well, of course." She turned and started up the stairs, her blond hair bouncing behind her.

I followed after her, thinking about basketball. I practice a lot, I told myself. I'm not going to let the team down.

We found my dad in the projection booth surrounded by whirring equipment. He glanced up from an enormous film reel and flashed us a smile.

Dad and I look a lot alike. We're both tall and a little chunky. We both have straight blond mop hair that can't be combed or brushed down.

"The movie is awesome the third time!" I told him. "Megan didn't like it, but I think it's the best one yet."

"I'm just about to start it again," Dad said. "Are you staying for the next show, Danny?"

I shook my head. "Mom said I have to get home."

I reached down and started to spin an empty metal wheel.

"Better not touch that," Dad warned. "It's a rewind spool. I need it to—"

"Hey—!" I cried out as the metal spool came spinning off its machine. It clattered to the floor and rolled across the narrow booth.

I dived after it.

"Danny—look out! Don't!"

I heard Dad's shout—too late.

I ran in front of the projector.
The beam of white light shot over me.
I felt its heat.
Blinding white. So bright and hot…
I stumbled forward, out of the light.
But I felt so strange. Dazed…
Dazed by the weird white light.

CHAPTER 3

The late Sunday afternoon sun floated low over the trees as I jogged up to the playground in my T-shirt and white basketball shorts. Long shadows stretched over the asphalt basketball court near the school building.

Coach Gray had called a weekend practice for the Tigers. The city tournament started soon, and we had to be ready for our big rival from across town, Stern Valley.

I didn't see the coach anywhere. But I saw Rommy and Jake and a couple of the other guys already warming up, dribbling in close and taking layup shots.

"It's the Danny-Man!" Rommy called. "Looking good!"

Jake flashed me a thumbs-up.

I trotted across the court. Rommy heaved a ball at me.

I caught it and began to dribble without slowing my pace. I drove toward him, faked right, faked left, and shot.

Air ball.

I didn't come close to touching the backboard.

"Coach isn't coming," Jake announced. "He's sick."

"We don't need him," Rommy said. "We already know the routine."

"Go, Tigers!" someone from the bleachers shouted. Shielding my eyes from the lowering sun, I saw a few kids scattered around up there. Nothing better to do but watch our practice, I guessed.

"Hey, Rommy—in-your-face time!" The shout came from a red-haired girl with her hands cupped around her mouth.

"Is that your little sister?" Jake asked Rommy.

Rommy nodded. "I'm supposed to be watching her. Just ignore her. She's a total geek."

The sun dipped lower. The shadows covered the basketball court. "Let's get started," I said, shivering.

The air wasn't cold. Why did I suddenly feel chilled?

I dribbled a ball from hand to hand. Through my legs. Faster. Then slower.

The ball felt heavy, as if it wasn't fully inflated. I had to hit it hard against the court to make it bounce back to my hand.

I shivered again. Hope I'm not getting sick, I thought.

I counted seven of us. Five starters and two subs. We did some other warm-up exercises, then lined up to practice foul shots.

Normally I'm a really accurate foul shooter. But for some reason today, my ball kept dying before it reached the basket.

"Energy!" Rommy called. "Energy, everybody. Get your energy up!"

He was pretending to be Coach Gray.

"Come on, Danny-Man. Slam it or jam it!"

We always finished our practices with a slam-dunk competition. A high pass—a high leap—we took turns sailing up over the net, slamming the ball down.

"Slam it or jam it!" I heard Rommy's sister shout from the bleachers.

"Does she know *anything* about basketball?" I asked him.

He shook his head. "I don't think so."

Who was that sitting at the very top row? Was it Megan?

I straightened my shorts and turned back in time to catch a high pass from Jake. "Look alive, Danny-Man!"

I dribbled around Rommy and passed the ball back to Jake. "Okay. Ready," I announced.

I usually win the slam-dunk contests. Even though the other players are all sixth graders, I'm the tallest guy on the team. I'm nearly five-eleven and still growing. Dad is six-two. He thinks I might grow even taller than he is.

Jake moved to the left of the basket, holding the ball waist high in both hands, preparing to pass.

I lined up at the foul line and took a deep breath. I bent my knees a few times, as if testing their springiness.

Then I took off.

Jake heaved the ball high.

I leaped up, up, up into the air to catch it and slam it down into the net.

"Owwww!" I screamed as my hands slapped the solid wood backboard under the basket.

The ball hit the bottom of the board and bounced away.

I dropped to the ground, both hands stinging. "Whoa."

"What happened, Danny?" Rommy came running over. "You missed by a mile."

"Uh…guess I jumped late," I said. I wiped away cold sweat from the back of my neck.

"You barely got off the ground."

"That's a do-over," I insisted. I bounced the ball to Jake. "Throw it higher this time. I'm going to *fly*."

My heart pounding, my hands still stinging, I made my way back to the foul line.

No big deal, Danny, I told myself.

You didn't time the jump right. It happens all the time.

I took a deep breath and let it out slowly. "Ready," I called to Jake.

I took off toward the basket.

Jake fired the ball high.

I jumped—and sailed up off the ground. Flying...flying high...

My hands grabbed for the ball—but it flew just out of reach. I grabbed nothing but air.

My jump took me only halfway up to the hoop.

And as I started to come down, I heard screams—screams and shrieks—from the bleachers.

CHAPTER 4

I landed off-balance. I stumbled and fell to my knees.

Something clung to my ankles.

Screams and laughter rang out from the bleachers behind me. And I heard Rommy's sister shouting, "No way! No way!"

I scrambled to my feet—and saw why the kids were shouting.

My shorts had fallen off.

I stared down at my underwear, then at the white basketball trunks around my ankles. I could feel my face grow hot. I knew I was blushing.

As I reached to pull up the shorts, I glimpsed Megan at the top of the bleachers. She was staring down at me through binoculars! What's with *that*? I wondered.

Rommy slapped my shoulder. He grinned at me. "Nice shot, ace. Let's see you do that again!"

Jake was still laughing, bending over, hands pressed against his knees.

I adjusted the shorts. They still felt loose around my waist. "The...uh...the elastic must be shot," I muttered.

I let go of the shorts, and they started to slip down again. No way I could practice.

"Catch you later, guys," I called.

Holding my shorts with one hand, I turned away from the court and started for home, walking quickly. I could still hear the shrieks and laughter repeating in my mind.

"Danny! Hey, wait up!"

I turned and saw Megan chasing after me, the binoculars bouncing in front of her as she ran.

I groaned. I didn't like the evil grin on her face.

She caught up to me, and the grin grew wider, those dimples at either end. "Are those your dad's shorts?"

I started walking faster. "Ha ha. You're a riot."

She started jogging to keep up. "You look shorter or something. Maybe that's why you couldn't jump so high."

"Don't be stupid," I muttered.

She snickered. "Maybe you're turning into Shrinkman."

"Maybe you're turning into a jerk," I said angrily.

I stomped up the driveway. I was in no mood for Megan and her dumb jokes. I started up the front stoop—and tripped on the step.

"Ow!" I scraped my knee on the concrete.

Why did the steps seem higher?

I turned back and saw Megan watching me, studying me.

What's going on? I wondered. Why do I feel so strange?

CHAPTER 5

I couldn't fall asleep that night. I was worried that I might be getting sick.

Maybe I'm coming down with the flu or something, I decided. That's why I couldn't jump as high as I usually do.

I climbed out of bed, turned on the light, and sat down at my drawing table. I pulled out a clean sheet of paper and started to pencil a new Shrinkman comic.

I thought for a minute or so. Then I lettered in the title: *Shrinkman Grows Up*. I started to draw the first panel. Shrinkman, the size of a mouse, is being attacked by a giant crow.

It was a pretty good drawing. But I kept yawning and my eyelids felt as heavy as steel.

So I turned off the light and wearily slipped back into bed.

The next morning I woke up on the floor beside my bed.

No big deal. It happens a lot. I always toss and turn in my sleep. I fall out of bed, and it doesn't even wake me up.

I sat up and pulled carpet fuzz from my hair. Then I climbed to my feet.

"Whoa!" My pajama bottoms fell to the floor.

"I don't believe this," I muttered.

I kicked the pajamas out of my way and started to get dressed. I pulled on a T-shirt and a pair of baggy jeans.

Wait a minute. The jeans were never *this* baggy. And why did the jean legs come down over my feet?

"You're turning into Shrinkman." Megan's words repeated in my ears.

That's totally dumb, I told myself.

But why didn't my jeans fit?

I crossed the room to the dresser mirror.

"Hey—!" Did somebody raise the mirror?

It has to be a joke, I realized.

That's it. Megan convinced my mom and dad to play along in one of her dumb jokes.

They raised the mirror. And put a pair of bigger jeans on top in my dresser.

They're tired of hearing about Shrinkman all the time. So they're trying to make me think that *I'm* shrinking.

All a joke, I told myself.

I tightened my belt a few notches to keep the jeans up.

Well, I can play along with it. I'm going to pretend I haven't noticed a thing, I decided.

I brushed my hair and hurried down to breakfast. As I entered the kitchen, I saw Megan sitting at the breakfast table. She's always at our house. The food is much better.

"Wow!" Her eyes grew wide when she looked at me. "Danny, are you losing weight?"

I'm not going to play along, I told myself.

"No. I'm fine," I replied. "Where's my mom and dad?"

"They told me to tell you they had to leave early this morning."

I sat down across from Megan and poured myself a glass of orange juice. Why did the carton feel so heavy?

"You look a little weird," Megan insisted. She studied me like some kind of insect specimen. If she had a magnifying glass, she would have raised it to her eye.

"No. I'm fine," I said again.

I'm fine. I'm fine. I repeated those words to myself.

But why did the orange juice glass look so much bigger? Had Mom and Dad switched glasses as part of the joke?

Wasn't that a lot of work for just a dumb joke?

I'm not going to say anything, I reminded myself. I'm going to pretend I don't notice a thing.

That will spoil the joke for them.

"Do you feel as if you're shrinking at all?" Megan asked.

I didn't answer. I ate breakfast in a hurry, grabbed my backpack—which seemed much bigger and heavier—and stepped out the door.

Things didn't get *really* scary until I walked into the school.

CHAPTER 6

I had to stand on tiptoe to get water from the water fountain in the front hall.

When I opened my locker, I stared up at the books on the top shelf. I couldn't reach them.

All the other kids suddenly seemed taller than me—even the third and fourth graders.

I had to tighten my belt another two notches to keep my jeans from falling. And I had to roll the cuffs up to keep from tripping over them.

I stepped into Miss Denver's classroom and gasped.

The desks all seemed so tall! I had to use both hands to climb up into my seat.

I suddenly felt cold all over. I felt sick. My stomach heaved. My throat tightened up. I struggled to breathe.

"It isn't a joke," I muttered to myself.

Something horrible is happening to me, I realized. Something horrible—and real.

I'm shrinking.

I'm shrinking like Shrinkman. Except he's a *cartoon* superhero. And he can get bigger whenever he wants.

I'm real. I'm a real person.

And I'm shrinking…shrinking fast.

I could see the other kids staring at me. At first they laughed. But when they realized it was me—a small me—they stopped laughing instantly. And their expressions changed to shock…and horror.

I can't stay here, I decided.

Not with everyone staring at me. Not with all my friends thinking I've become some kind of freak.

I can't just sit at this big desk and shrink away to nothing.

I've got to get help.

I turned in the seat and lowered myself to the floor. The bell hadn't rung yet. Kids were still walking into the classroom. They all gaped at me in shock as I made my way to the door.

"What happened to Danny?" I heard someone whisper.

"Is that his little brother?"

For some reason, I suddenly thought about the basketball game against Stern Valley. The other guys were counting on me. But now I was a shrimp. How could I help them out?

I pictured Rommy picking me up by the waist and holding me high so that I could shoot a basket.

The thought made me start to tremble. My legs shook so hard, I could barely walk.

Slowly I made my way down the hall to the nurse's office. She greeted me with a surprised gasp and jumped up from behind her desk. "Danny?"

"I—I don't feel well," I stammered, my voice tiny and weak. "Can I call my parents?"

"Of course." She shoved the phone across her desk toward me. I had to stand on tiptoe to punch in the number.

I dialed Dad at work. It took a long time for him to come to the phone. "Danny, what's wrong?"

I was never so glad to hear his voice. "I don't... feel so well. Do you think you could come pick me up?"

Mom came home from work, too. When Dad and I pulled up the driveway, she came running out to greet us.

She pulled open my car door—and screamed. Then she pressed her hands against the sides of her face. "But you were fine yesterday..."

"We'll call Dr. Hayward. I'm sure he'll agree to see us right away," Dad said.

I saw him exchange worried glances with Mom. I saw tears glimmer in Mom's eyes. She quickly wiped them away.

"Why is this happening?" I asked. "Real people don't shrink. Only guys in comic books or movies."

"Dr. Hayward will be able to explain," Dad said.

Mom swallowed hard and wiped away more tears.

They helped me up the steep front steps and into the house. Mom hurried to the phone to call the doctor.

Hands on my shoulders, Dad led me over to the wall beside the kitchen pantry. I could see the pencil marks on the wall where we had marked my height every few months. The marks went up to five-foot-eight.

I turned and pressed my back against the wall. I couldn't stop from trembling. Dad chewed his bottom lip as he studied the marks. He left the room for a second, then returned with a tape measure. He didn't say a word as he stretched out the tape.

"Well?" I asked. "How tall? How much have I shrunk?"

Dad frowned at the tape measure. His eyes kept going from the new marks on the wall he'd just made and back to me.

"Come on, Dad," I pleaded. "What does it say?"

Dad cleared his throat. "You're three feet tall, Danny."

"What—?" Mom let out a shriek.

"No!" I cried.

Dad squeezed my shoulder. "Let's not panic. I'm sure there's a good explanation. I'm sure—"

"Dr. Hayward said to bring you right now," Mom said.

"If I keep shrinking this fast, I'll disappear in a day or two!" I wailed.

Dad guided me toward the door. "Come on. Let's go. The doctor will know what to do."

"Are you sure, Dad? What if he doesn't?" I asked. "What if he doesn't?"

CHAPTER 7

"I've never seen anything like it," Dr. Hayward said, shaking his head.

Dr. Hayward is young and good-looking with bright green eyes under thick blond eyebrows. His wavy blond hair is always brushed straight back off his tanned forehead.

I've always thought Dr. Hayward looks more like a lifeguard at the beach than a doctor. But he must be very good because his waiting room is always jammed with people.

But we didn't have to wait today.

As soon as he saw me, he ushered me into the examining room. And now I sat on the hard metal table in just my underwear as he shook his head, sweeping a hand back through his wavy hair.

"Do you feel strange in any way, Danny?"

I cleared my throat. "Just scared."

"Headaches? Upset stomach?"

"Not really," I said.

He nodded solemnly. "Didn't you once tell me about some superhero you liked to draw? A superhero who could shrink?"

"Yes. Shrinkman," I said. "But you don't think—"

"No," he interrupted. "Just an odd coincidence."

He pulled open a drawer and lifted a stethoscope.

I'm going to do a complete examination. We'll do a blood work-up. And we'll take X-rays. And we'll see what shows up."

"Am I...going to keep shrinking?" I asked.

"I can't really answer that, Danny. Wish I could. My guess is that this is something glandular."

"Glandular? What does that mean?"

"I'll explain later. Let's get started." He pressed the stethoscope against my chest.

I shivered. Why are they always so cold?

He pressed it all over my chest and throat and back, listening intently. Then he poked a light into my ears and studied them for a long while. He checked my throat and studied my eyes.

His expression remained grim. The blond eyebrows arched tensely over his green eyes. He didn't make a sound.

A nurse came in, tapped my arm a few times, and tied a blue plastic cord around it. "You can look away if you want to," she said, raising a hypodermic syringe.

"It's okay," I replied.

She jabbed the needle into my arm. I watched the dark red blood flow into the glass vial. She filled four vials before she pulled the needle out.

"We need to do a brain scan," Dr. Hayward said. "Then I want to send you for other brain tests."

My mouth dropped open. "You don't think that this is all in my *mind*, do you?"

The doctor handed me my shirt. "Of course not. I'm just looking for a clue, any kind of clue as to what is causing this growth loss."

He turned and pulled a glass bottle from a cabinet. He twisted off the cap and poured a thick blue liquid into a glass. "Drink this down."

I raised the glass to my mouth, but then quickly lowered it. It smelled horrible! Like skunk juice. "What is it?"

"It's a kind of ink, Danny. When you drink it, we'll be able to follow it through your system on an X-ray machine."

He pushed the glass toward my face. "Go ahead. Bottoms up. Hold your nose while you drink. It might help get it down."

I held my breath and pressed the glass to my lips. The liquid poured onto my tongue, thick as motor oil.

"This stuff is so *gross*," I gagged. But I pinched my nose and choked it down.

Dr. Hayward smiled at me. "Very good. Now get dressed, Danny. I'm sending you to a lab across town for the X-rays. I'll go explain everything to your parents while you get dressed."

"But…when will we know what's wrong?" I asked, the disgusting taste of the thick blue liquid lingering in my mouth.

"We'll have the tests back in two or three days," he replied. "Then we might be able to explain…" His voice trailed off.

"Two or three *days*?" I cried. "But—but—I could *disappear* by then!"

His blue eyes seemed to fade. He patted my trembling shoulder. "We'll make sure someone keeps an eye on you."

The X-rays and brain scans and tests took all day.

At the end of it I was so exhausted, I could barely move or speak. Dad drove us home. Mom held me on her lap like a baby.

"Don't worry, Danny," Mom said. "Dr. Hayward will find out what's wrong with you. Then he'll figure out how to turn things around."

She was trying to sound brave. But her voice quivered, and tears bubbled up in her eyes once again.

Dad turned the car into the driveway, and I saw someone sitting on the front lawn.

Megan?

Yes. She waved to us. And I realized she wasn't sitting—she was standing!

"Look!" she cried. "Danny—do you believe it? Look! I'm shrinking, too!"

CHAPTER 8

I jumped out of the car and ran across the grass to her. "Megan—how did it happen?"

To my surprise, she started to laugh.

I stopped with a gasp when I saw she had her shoes strapped to her knees. Her legs stretched on the grass behind her.

All a joke. All a stupid joke.

"Get up, Megan!" I shrieked. I grabbed her arm and tried to tug her to her feet. "It's not funny! It's *not!*"

Mom hurried up to us, her expression stern. "Megan, what are you doing?" she asked sharply.

"Sorry, Mrs. Marin. I just—" Megan grabbed her shoes off the grass and climbed quickly to her feet. "I didn't mean—"

"We have a very serious problem here," Mom told her. "It isn't a joking matter. It's very frightening and...and..."

Mom bit her lip to keep from crying. She placed a hand on my shoulder and started to guide me to the house. "We'd better go inside. Good-bye, Megan."

"I'm sorry," Megan repeated, following after us. "Could I come in? I'd like to talk to you. I—"

"I don't think it's a good idea," Mom said. "Some other time, Megan."

"But, Mrs. Marin, I want to apologize. I really—"

Mom cut Megan off. "Danny has had a very rough day. I'm sure you do feel bad. But I think he should be with us now."

She pulled open the front door.

I heard a shrill bark.

No time to move. No time to get out of the way.

"No—Rocky!" I screamed.

Our big Irish setter, barking happily, burst out of the house to greet us. He leaped high—and his front paws came crashing down on my shoulders.

I was too small to stand up to him. He outweighed me now. And when he stood up, he towered over me. I fell back, fell off the stoop.

I landed hard on my back on the concrete walk.

Long red tail wagging furiously, Rocky jumped on top of me.

"No, Rocky! No!" Mom screamed.

"He's *crushing* me!" I shrieked.

So heavy...he was so heavy...

"Helllp! Get him off!"

Mom and Megan were screaming, too.

I raised my arms to shield myself as Rocky jumped again.

I saw a fast-moving shadow. Then realized it was Dad.

He stepped between the charging dog and me.

Rocky gleefully leaped up, his front paws hitting Dad's chest. "Good boy. Good Rocky!" Dad cried.

Holding on to the dog, he turned to me. "Get into the house, Danny. We'll have to keep Rocky in the garage until...until you're normal-sized again."

He was petting Rocky, holding him by the collar. "He's just happy to see you. He doesn't realize..."

"I know," I said. I hurried to the house, following Mom. I had to run to keep up with her.

"Danny, I have to talk to you," Megan called. She said something else, but Rocky's excited barks drowned her out.

Mom helped me back up the steep steps and into the house. I wanted to answer Megan, but Mom closed the front door after us.

I let out a long sigh of relief. "Rocky is just too big," I said. "Why don't we have a nice, little wiener dog?"

Mom didn't smile. She had a hand clenching her chin. Her head was tilted as she studied me. "Danny, go stand next to the marks in the hall."

The back of my neck prickled. "Why? We just measured me this morning, remember?"

"Don't argue," she replied sharply.

I sighed again and made my way to the wall. I backed up against it, standing beside the pencil marks.

My legs began to tremble. My shoulders still ached from where Rocky's paws had landed on me.

I didn't like the grim expression on Mom's face as she studied the pencil marks.

I heard a tiny cry escape her throat. "Danny— I'm so sorry. So sorry."

"Huh? Why, Mom?"

She shook her head sadly. Her eyes glistened with tears. "You're two inches shorter."

I groaned. "Oh no. Mom—what are we going to do?"

She shook her head and didn't reply.

"Mom?" I had to reach up really high to grab her hand. It was cold and wet. "Mom?"

She squeezed my hand. She turned her head away.

I guessed she didn't want me to see her crying.

THE ADVENTURES OF SHRINKMAN

I took a deep breath. Two inches shorter? From this morning?

Why was this happening to me?

Why?

CHAPTER 9

I decided to go upstairs and try to do some home-work. I needed something to think about besides shrinking.

Before I could sit at my desk, I had to stack two phone books on my desk chair. Then I grabbed the chair arms and hoisted myself up.

When I sat down to face the computer, I had to stretch as far as I could to turn it on.

The keyboard suddenly appeared as wide as a piano. Tapping my fingers on the desktop, I waited impatiently for the computer to boot up.

My tiny hand barely fit around the mouse. I moved and clicked until the speakers buzzed and the monitor screen lit up.

I don't know how long I sat there. An hour. Maybe two. Staring at the computer. Forcing myself to concentrate. But it was useless.

I'll go downstairs and get a snack, I thought. Then I'll come back and try again.

I started to lower myself from the phone books.

But the floor suddenly seemed a long way down.

I must have shrunk even more.

I'm too small to get out of the chair!

"Help!" I screamed. "Mom! Dad! Somebody— help me!"

Dad came running in. His mouth dropped open when he saw me sitting there.

He quickly tried to cover up his fear. Too late. I'd already seen the horror on his face.

"I've shrunk more—haven't I?" I said as he lifted me off the phone books on my desk chair.

He nodded solemnly. "I—I think you have, Danny."

He carried me downstairs and measured me against the wall. Then he shook his head sadly. Mom stood behind him, the color draining from her face.

"Well? Give me the bad news," I insisted, trying to be brave. My voice came out tiny and high, like a five-year-old's. My heart fluttered against my chest.

"Two feet," Dad replied in a whisper. "You're two feet tall now, Danny."

I gasped.

Mom stepped forward quickly. She had her hands clenched into tight fists. A tissue was balled up in one fist. Tear stains streaked her cheeks.

"Let's call Dr. Hayward," she said to Dad. "Maybe he has some news for us."

Mom told Dad Dr. Hayward's number, and he punched it in. He waited a long time. I could hear ring after ring.

"I'm getting a message tape," Dad said, frowning. "There's no one in the office."

He left a message, asking Dr. Hayward to call us right away. Then he turned off the phone and stared at me. "Where do you want to sleep, Danny? Maybe we could put together a little bed for you."

"No," I interrupted. "I want to sleep in my own bed." I swallowed hard. I suddenly remembered those movies I'd seen on TV—the one about the shrinking man who has to live in a dollhouse and the one about the father who accidentally shrinks his kids and they get lost in the backyard.

I used to think those movies were funny.

But now I didn't.

"Just don't lose me, okay?" I whispered. "Don't let me out of your sight."

"Of course we won't lose you!" Mom cried. She picked me up and hugged me.

But how long will they be able to see me? I wondered as we headed up to my bedroom.

Mom and Dad tucked me tightly into my bed. I sank into the pillow. It was nearly as tall as I was!

They left a dresser lamp on so they could see me easily. "We'll look in on you every few hours," Mom promised. When she kissed me good night, I felt like a little baby.

I was the *size* of a little baby!

They tiptoed out, and I shut my eyes. I felt very tired, but I was afraid to go to sleep.

What if I shrink down to the size of a bug?

What if I completely disappear during the night?

I tossed and turned for what seemed like hours. Worrying. Worrying about shrinking down to nothing. Worrying about disappearing forever.

CHAPTER 10

Shafts of pale yellow light slipped through the bedroom blinds. Slanted down over the darkness.

Woolly, gray blobs, like headless sheep, dotted the ground.

I squinted into the light, my heart pounding, my whole body trembling in terror.

My body?

I glanced down at my hands, my legs, my bare feet, toes poking from my baggy pajama bottoms.

"I haven't disappeared!" I cried out loud. My voice came out in a tiny mouse squeak.

I hadn't shrunk to nothing. But where was I?

The gray blobs glimmered in the shafts of light. Sunlight, I realized.

I raised my eyes to an enormous structure of wood and dark cloth. It loomed over me like an airplane hangar.

I stared at it for several seconds before I realized I was gazing up at my bed.

Tossing and turning, I had fallen out of bed during the night. And now I stood on my dark carpet surrounded by dust balls as big as cactuses. My bed so high above me I couldn't see the pillow or the sheets.

With a sick sigh, I gazed down at the floor.

I must be about the size of a parakeet, I realized.

I'm shrinking faster and faster. I'm only three or four inches tall!

How will anyone find me down here?

I didn't have long to think about the question.

I heard the thunder of footsteps. So loud I raised my hands to my ears. The floorboards shook. My tiny feet bounced on the carpet.

"Danny?"

I recognized Megan's voice. It boomed into my room as if on a loudspeaker cranked all the way up.

"Danny? Are you awake?"

Her shouts made my eardrums throb. The sound seemed to explode in my head.

More thundering footsteps. A shadow fell over me, blocking all the shafts of sunlight.

I saw two enormous white sneakers, as big as cars. They stopped at the foot of the bed.

"Danny? Where are you? Are you in here?"

I pressed my hands harder over my ears. Her calls were too loud. My head felt about to break open.

"Megan—I'm down here," I squeaked. My voice was so tiny and faint. "Can you hear me? I'm down here."

The big sneakers thudded closer.

I could see white socks poking up above the sneakers. I struggled to see Megan's face. But she was as tall as a mountain. I couldn't see that high.

"Megan—look down! Look down here!" I pleaded, screaming as hard as I could.

"Danny, are you hiding?" she called.

She didn't hear me. And she didn't see me.

And now she was moving toward me. CLUMP CLUMP CLUMP. The enormous shoes. Like army tanks.

"No—please!" I cried. "Megan—look out!"

I started to run out of the way.

I saw the sneaker rise up. Saw the rutted, gray sole float over me.

"Megan—noooooo!"

I raised my hands to protect myself as the heavy shoe tilted down over me. Lower…

Lower…

I gazed up at it, gritting my teeth, trembling in horror—and prepared to be crushed.

CHAPTER 11

"Noooooo—!" I threw myself onto the floor. And landed hard on my stomach. Spun over instantly. Spun again.

And rolled under the bed.

I heard the thunderous crash of the sneaker hitting the floor.

CLUMP. CLUMP. Megan walked quickly, searching for me.

"Megan—down here!"

How could I get her attention?

"Megan—?"

A corner of the bedsheet drooped nearly to the floor. Maybe…maybe I could grab it and pull myself onto the bed.

I raised both hands and jumped. I made a frantic grab for the sheet.

Missed.

I landed back on the carpet. Turning, I saw Megan starting to leave the room.

"No—wait! Please wait!" I pleaded.

I leaped again—and my hands wrapped around the corner of the sheet. Grasping it tightly, wrapping my legs around it, I struggled to pull myself up.

Up, up—an inch at a time.

But no. I wasn't strong enough. My arms were as thin as bird legs. With a furious cry, I started to fall.

I saw a blur of movement. Something wrapped around my chest and waist.

"Danny—?" I heard Megan's startled cry.

She had her fingers wrapped around me. She raised me to her face. Her enormous face. I felt as if I were peering at a huge billboard of Megan!

A cartoon I had seen many times on TV flashed into my mind. I pictured a laughing giant holding a trembling little mouse between his thumb and forefinger.

"Danny?" Megan's dark eyes were as big as basketballs. "You—you're so tiny!"

"Don't squeeze so hard!" I begged.

Her fingers loosened around my waist.

She could hear me!

Her mouth dropped open in amazement. It was like staring into a dark cave. Her teeth hung down from her giant lips, lips as big as house shingles.

"I don't believe it!" Megan exclaimed, holding me close to her face. So close I thought for a moment she was going to *swallow* me!

"Please whisper," I begged. "You're so loud. Everything is so loud."

"Sorry," she whispered. "You're so cute. Like a little bird."

"I don't feel cute," I snapped. "I'm really scared, Megan. You almost stepped on me before. And if I get any smaller…" My voice trailed off.

She lowered me away from her face. Her huge eyes continued to stare.

She raised something in her other hand. It took me a moment to recognize it. I saw fat metal bars. It looked like a prison cell.

"A birdcage?" I cried.

Megan nodded. "I brought it from my house. Remember my canary, George? He used to live in it."

"But—but I'm not a canary!" I protested.

Gripping me around the waist, she lowered me to the open cage door. "It's for keeping you safe, Danny," she whispered. "You just told me I almost stepped on you."

She set me down in the cage. The metal floor felt cold against my bare feet. I held my pajama bottoms up with both hands.

"I told your parents I was bringing it," Megan said. She closed the cage door. "They thought it was a good idea."

I peered up at her through the bars. "Megan, what am I going to do? Am I just going to disappear forever?"

"We won't let that happen," she said softly. "You'll be safe in here, Danny. And everyone can keep an eye on you."

I sat cross-legged on the cage floor, my back pressed between two thick metal bars. Megan carried me down to the kitchen.

Mom and Dad were sitting at the breakfast table, white mugs of coffee in their hands. They both jumped up when they saw Megan carry in the cage.

"He's in here," Megan said, setting the cage on the table. "I had a lot of trouble finding him."

Mom gasped. She covered her mouth with one hand.

Dad's mouth dropped open.

"You've got to *do* something!" I squeaked, standing and staring out at them, gripping the bars like a prisoner. "I'm shrinking fast!"

They didn't have time to reply. The phone rang.

The deafening sound echoed off the metal bars of my cage.

Mom and Dad both dived for the phone. Dad reached it first. "Hello?"

He turned to Mom. "It's Dr. Hayward."

I heard Dad repeat into the phone, "Yes...Yes... Yes..."

My heart thudded in my chest. My hands were suddenly ice-cold. I poked my head out between the bars, trying to hear.

Finally Dad set down the phone. He exchanged a long glance with Mom.

Mom's chin trembled. She bit her bottom lip.

"What did he say?" I called. "What did Dr. Hayward say?"

CHAPTER 12

"He wants to see us," Dad replied. "Right away."

"That's good news!" I cried. "That means he's found a cure—right?"

Mom and Dad exchanged another glance.

"Maybe," Dad said.

"He wouldn't bring us in unless he had good news for us," Mom added, forcing a smile. "Are you hungry, Danny? Let me give you a quick breakfast. Then we'll go hear what Dr. Hayward has to say."

I was too nervous and excited to feel hungry. I couldn't wait to hear Dr. Hayward's cure. I couldn't wait to grow back to normal size.

But when Mom slipped half a strawberry into the cage, I ate it hungrily. I broke off pieces and shoved them into my mouth.

Of course, I couldn't eat an entire half a strawberry. I felt full after only a few bites.

"I'll back the car out of the garage," Dad said, making his way to the kitchen door. "And I'll make sure Rocky has food and water. Then we'll go."

"I'd better get to school," Megan said, picking up her backpack from the counter. "I'm already late. It's been crazy at school, Danny. Tonight is the fifth grade Science Fair. Everyone has been going nuts trying to get all the projects finished."

"I'm sure you'll win, Megan," I called out of the cage.

A strange smile spread over her face. Her dark eyes flashed. "Yes. I'm sure I will, Danny."

She turned to my mom. "Call me as soon as you get back home, okay? Everyone at school is dying to hear that Danny will be okay."

Megan hurried out the door.

Mom leaned down, bringing her face close to me. I could see that her eyes were red. She looked pale and tense. I guessed that she hadn't slept much the night before.

"Have you finished your breakfast, Danny?" She pulled the chunk of leftover strawberry out. "Here. Have some orange juice. Then we'll go."

She slid a sewing thimble into the cage. It was filled to the top with orange juice.

I picked it up in both hands and took a few sips. "Enough," I said. "Come on. Let's get going. I can't wait to hear Dr. Hayward's good news."

"M–me, too," Mom replied, removing the thimble and pushing the cage door closed.

She lifted the cage by the handle. The cage floor rocked, and I fell to my knees. I dropped to a sitting position and held on tight to the swinging perch above my head. The cage bounced and tilted as Mom carried it outside.

The bright sunlight shooting through the cage bars made me squint.

I heard a deafening roar and realized it was the car backing out of the garage.

Mom started to jog across the lawn to the car.

The cage bounced harder.

I lost my grip on the wooden perch.

I started to slide over the metal floor.

And, to my horror, *the cage door flew open!*

"No—!" I made a frantic grab for the bars.

Missed.

The cage bounced hard—and I went sailing out the open door.

I dropped to the asphalt driveway. I screamed all the way down.

I landed hard on my elbows and knees. And turned instantly toward the car. "Mom—!"

Did she see that I had fallen out of the cage?

No.

I watched her slide into the passenger seat. She set the cage down in her lap.

"Mom—nooooo!" I shrieked. "Can't you hear me? I fell out! Mom—stop! I fell out!"

The passenger door slammed shut.

I jumped to my feet and waved frantically with both hands. "Mom—wait! Wait!" I screeched at the top of my lungs.

I stared frozen in the middle of the driveway, praying they would notice, praying they would see the empty cage.

But no.

The car idled for a few moments. Then it started to move. Started to back down the drive. The chrome bumper flashed in my eyes. The huge black tires made a grinding sound.

And I realized I was about to be run over!

CHAPTER 13

Roadkill.

The word flashed in my mind.

I dropped facedown on the drive. The hot asphalt burned my skin.

I tucked my arms beneath me. Shut my eyes…

…And the car rolled over me, chugging, grinding, roaring.

Something on the bottom of the car scraped my back. But the car passed over me. The fat, black tires missed by inches.

"Sometimes it *helps* to be the size of a bird," I muttered to myself.

Breathing hard, sweat pouring down my face, I leaped to my feet. Spun around. Again, I waved frantically at the car and shouted for them to come back.

But they still hadn't realized the cage was empty.

I watched, trembling, as our blue Taurus backed into the street, then roared away.

"Now what?" I asked myself.

I've got to get to Dr. Hayward's office. I have to be cured by him before I disappear completely.

But how can I get there?

If my parents came back, how would they be able to find me?

I didn't have time to think of answers.

I heard a low growl.

I turned to the open garage.

And saw Rocky come trotting out, his back arched, teeth bared...his eyes on *me*.

CHAPTER 14

The big dog lowered his head, snarling a warning. He pulled back his lips, revealing two rows of teeth.

I cupped my hands around my mouth. "Rocky—it's me!" I shouted. "Rocky—it's Danny!"

My cry didn't settle him down. He began to bark furiously. He snapped his jaw, dark eyes glaring.

"Rocky—no!" I yelled. "Don't you recognize me? Can't you *smell* me?"

Growling again, the Irish setter took a few more steps toward me. From down on the driveway, he looked as big as a horse!

Was he going to trample me?

Or chew me to bits?

Once, a few years ago, Rocky carried a dead mouse into the kitchen. He had ripped it apart with his paws and teeth. I watched him bite the mouse's head off. I still remembered the sick *crunch* it made.

Rocky stared down at me, eyes narrowing, snapping his jaw menacingly.

I swallowed hard, my stomach lurching.

Now I'm the mouse…

He hesitated for a second, sniffing hard.

"Rocky—listen to me! Down, boy! Down!"

He uttered one more sharp bark. .

Then he raised both giant front paws—and leaped.

I raised my hands to fight him off. But I wasn't strong enough to push the huge dog away. He lowered his head. Snapped his jaw around me—and lifted me into the air in his teeth.

"No, Rocky! Noooooo!" I screamed.

He tossed me into the air. I sailed up over the Irish setter's head and fell back onto the driveway.

"Owwwww!" I landed hard on my shoulder. Pain shot down my body.

Before I could move, I saw his big head lowering again. His mouth opened wide and his teeth closed around me.

Hot, sticky saliva clung to my face, my arms.

Grunting loudly, the dog clamped his teeth tighter over me.

Then he tossed me up again.

A trail of saliva flew behind me as I sailed up, then back to the driveway. I hit harder this time. Skidded on my stomach.

He's playing with me! I realized.

He's just playing now. But what is he going to do when he's finished playing?

Again, I pictured the mouse in Rocky's mouth. Again, I heard the crunch of its head being bitten off.

I scrambled to my feet and tried to dive into the flowerbed at the side of the driveway.

But Rocky was too fast for me. He picked me up in his teeth again. Swung me around. Swung me like one of his pull-rope toys.

And as I hung helplessly in his mouth, dripping, sticky with saliva, frozen in terror, I saw another dog come running across the yard.

A large yellow dog. Teeth bared, head down for the attack, it bounded rapidly over the grass, taking long strides.

Tightening his grip on me, Rocky growled at the newcomer.

The yellow dog growled back.

To my shuddering horror, I realized they were about to fight over me.

CHAPTER 15

With a furious snarl, Rocky spun away from the other dog.

The yellow dog leaped forward. I let out a scream as his jaw snapped at my feet.

Growling, panting hard, Rocky sat back on his haunches.

The yellow dog made another leap for me.

This time his teeth dug into my ankles.

I screamed again as a wave of pain swept over me.

Oh no! It's a tug of war.

The two dogs snarled menacingly at each other, pawing the ground, as they took turns sinking their teeth into my skin.

With a frantic effort, I reached up both hands. I grabbed Rocky's snout. And I pinched as hard as I could, squeezing the tender, soft part.

Rocky let out a startled squeal.

His jaw slid open, and I sailed out of his mouth.

Dripping and sticky, I hit the driveway running. I dived into the flowerbed and hid under a clump of fat, green leaves.

I could hear Rocky sniffing hard. I saw his shadow sweep over the flowerbed.

I peeked out and watched him sniff at the yellow dog. Then, to my relief, the two of them loped off toward the backyard, trotting side by side.

Thank goodness dogs have such short attention spans, I thought.

I rubbed dog saliva off my chin and neck and checked myself out. I had a few cuts on my legs, but nothing serious. My pajamas were soaked and torn to shreds. I wiped my bare feet off with a leaf.

I peered out to make sure the coast was clear. Then I made my way through the flowerbed to the front lawn.

I sighed, realizing I must have shrunk even more. The blades of grass came up over my waist. Now I'm the size of a sparrow, I decided.

How can I ever get to Dr. Hayward's office?

I shielded my eyes with one hand and looked down the street. Our front lawn suddenly appeared to be a mile long!

I'm going to need help, I saw. I can't get all the way across town by myself. It would take years!

I heard the rumble of a car. My heart started to race. Was it Mom and Dad? Did they come back for me?

I stood on tiptoe to see over some tall grass. I let out a disappointed sigh as a red minivan roared past.

Maybe I can make it to a bus stop, I told myself. Maybe I can hop onto the crosstown bus. It will take me really close to the doctor's office.

It seemed like a plan.

I started to make my way toward the street, pushing the blades of grass out of my way with both hands.

I had gone only four or five steps when I heard a clattering sound from nearby.

A rustling, scratching sound.

I stopped to listen.

The curtain of grass in front of me suddenly parted.

And a figure lurched forward. A green stick figure.

A grasshopper.

Nearly as tall as me, it rose up, clicking its stick legs. It opened a round mouth and spit a gooey, black blob onto my chest.

"Owww!" I cried out, more startled than hurt.

Searching desperately for a hiding place or an escape route, I tried to back away.

But the grasshopper moved quickly.

Its slender body arched up in front of me. It raised a gleaming, green leg.

It swung the leg and slapped me. Slapped me so hard, I toppled to the ground.

And then it scrabbled over me, lowering its head to my throat, moving in for the kill.

CHAPTER 16

Frantically I grabbed one of the insect's legs with both hands. It felt warm and hard as a lobster claw. Gripping the leg, I pulled myself up off the ground and swung out from under the creature.

It opened its round mouth and spit again. But this time the sticky, black blob shot past my face.

With all my strength I tugged on the insect's leg. Tugged hard until I pulled it down to the ground. Then I dived onto its hard, spiny back. As I struggled to shove its head into the dirt, I felt a rumbling beneath me.

The grasshopper's wings shot out. They fluttered rapidly and sent me sailing off the insect's back, facedown onto the grass.

Pulling myself to my knees, I heard the grasshopper snap its legs. The snapping sound reminded me of celery cracking.

It suddenly dipped low, then came hopping at me, leaping high off the ground.

I tried to crawl out of its way.

But it came too fast.

Its front legs stung my back. It felt like darts plunging through my skin.

I cried out and struggled to roll away.

But the big insect stung me again. Slapped my face with the bone-hard legs. Stung my chest. My arms.

Reeling in pain, I rolled away.

And to my surprise, started to fall.

Down a steep dirt tunnel. A hole in the ground?

I toppled down the damp, dark dirt, rolling over and over. Rolling away from sunlight. Falling into a deep darkness.

I landed on my back. Landed on something soft.

Landed on something alive!

CHAPTER 17

I felt warm bodies pulsating beneath me. My body bobbed up and down on their wavelike motion.

Something scratched my face. I felt something heavy crawl onto my chest.

I tried to stand up. But I was on top of a sea of living creatures moving rapidly. I fell back to my knees.

And felt the prickle of tiny feet as *something crawled onto my back.*

Gripped in horror, I struggled to stand again.

What were these creatures? How far into the ground had I fallen?

A flash of sunlight—like a bolt of lightning—answered my question.

In the brief second of light I saw the giant ant on my chest, the ants on the tunnel walls, the carpet of ants beneath me.

Ants as big as dogs!

I felt a wave of terror sweep down my body. I opened my mouth to scream—and one of the ants stuck its hairy, round head into my mouth!

Choking, gagging, I shoved it away.

I could taste the creature on my tongue. Metallic tasting and sour.

My disgust gave me new strength.

I grabbed an ant on my stomach and flung it aside. Then I began crawling frantically, grabbing ants and pushing them out of my way, my knees scrabbling over their soft, warm backs.

I elbowed ants away. Shook one off the back of my neck. Plucked one off my leg.

I crawled till I landed on dirt. Then, digging my hands into the soft, damp earth, I pulled myself up, up, up the ant hole, scrambled up like an insect searching for light.

Yes! I made it. Into the bright sunshine. Surrounded by the glowing grass of the front yard.

I stood and brushed the dirt off my hands, off my face, off my shredded pajamas. Then I gazed down the lawn to the street, so far away.

I don't care how far it is, I decided. I don't care how long it takes. I'm going to make it to the street. And I'm going to make it to Dr. Hayward's office to get my cure.

I stared at my bare feet, dirt-stained and scratched. If only I had shoes...

But who makes shoes for a boy the size of a mouse?

Shoving grass blades out of my way, I began to push through the lawn, heading to the street. I felt as if I were walking through a thick jungle.

I don't know how much time passed. But my arms and legs ached and throbbed, and my whole body was drenched with sweat when I finally reached the curb.

I jumped off the sidewalk and into the street.

The hot road burned my toes. But I didn't care.

"If I can make it to the street," I told myself, stopping to catch my breath, "I can make it to the bus stop."

I turned and began walking quickly, keeping the curb—high as a cement wall—close at my right.

I wiped sweat off my face, then shielded my eyes with one hand from the bright sun. It was high in the sky when I finally reached the bus stop on the corner. The pavement shimmered like silver.

Two women carrying large shopping bags stood at the bus stop, waiting for the blue-and-white city bus.

I pulled myself up onto the curb. Then I hid behind a soda can someone had tossed on the grass and waited.

A few minutes later the bus rolled up, squealing to a stop. I stepped out from behind the soda can— and my heart sank.

The bus rose up into the sky, as tall as a skyscraper.

The door hissed open. The first woman began to climb on.

And I stared in horror at the first step. *Miles* over my head.

No way I could jump onto it. Or even reach it to pull myself up. I needed help.

I ran up beside the second woman. I gazed at her long blond hair trailing behind her white blouse, down to her tight-fitting blue denim jeans. She seemed a mile high, too!

"Help me!" I cried, cupping my hands around my mouth. "Please—can you help me onto the bus?"

She didn't hear me. She raised her left shoe onto the bottom step and reached for the handrail.

"Please!" I screamed.

She raised her other shoe to the bottom step—and dropped her bus token. I saw it roll off the bus onto the curb.

I jumped out of its way. The token was as big as a manhole cover!

The woman turned, stepped off the bus, and bent down to pick up the token.

My last chance, I realized.

A desperate idea flashed into my mind.

I'll jump onto her leg. I'll grab her jeans and hold on tight, and she'll carry me onto the bus.

Muttering to herself, she pulled the token from the grass. Then she turned and started back to the bus.

I took a deep breath and began to run.

I saw her raise her right foot onto the bottom bus step.

Picking up speed, my bare feet slapping the sidewalk, I shot out both hands.

Leaped high at her left leg.

Grabbed for the jeans…

…and missed.

CHAPTER 18

"Ohhhh." A horrified cry burst from my chest.

My hands hit air.

I started to slide down the woman's leg.

She raised her foot onto the bus step. As I fell, I heard the loud *clang* of the token dropping into the token box.

I landed with a thud on her white sneaker—and frantically grabbed the laces.

I wrapped both hands around the laces and held on tight as she bumped—bumped—bumped—up the steps, onto the bus. I rode her sneaker like a bucking bronco in a rodeo.

My knuckles turned white as I gripped the laces tighter. Held on as she made her way down the aisle and took a seat across from the rear exit.

"Yessss!" I cried happily. I wanted to pump my fists in the air. But I was terrified of falling off the sneaker.

The bus roared as it pulled away from the curb. I gazed toward the front. I could only see under the seats. The bus stretched for miles, like an ocean liner.

"Whoa—!" I cried out in surprise as the woman started to cross her legs.

I saw her right foot swing over toward the left.

About to be crushed, I let go of the shoelaces and dived to the bus floor. I rolled under the seat to safety. And clung to the metal chair leg the rest of the way.

Hours later, when I stepped up to the glass front door of Dr. Hayward's office, I nearly cried. I felt so happy, so relieved, so *exhausted*.

Jumping off the bottom step of the bus had been the most terrifying experience of my life. If you didn't count being used in a tug-of-war between two dogs, fighting a grasshopper, or falling into the middle of an ant colony.

Crossing the busiest street in town wasn't exactly a picnic, either. I scurried across in terror, looking like a frightened squirrel.

Now here I stood in front of Dr. Hayward's office. My next challenge was to get through the door.

I had to wait a long time for a normal-sized person to come out. Then I had to dart inside before the door slammed shut on me.

I stepped into the waiting room and gazed up at the chairs and couches. Empty. No one waiting.

Where were Mom and Dad?

Miles above me the fish tank gurgled softly. I felt my stomach start to gurgle, too. I suddenly felt sick.

Didn't my parents wait for me? Where were they?

I heard a cough at the front of the room. I saw Carla, Dr. Hayward's assistant, sitting behind the skyscraper-high reception desk.

I ran under the coffee table and up to her desk, calling to her. But she was talking into the phone. "I'm sorry, the doctor will be out of town that week…" She didn't hear me.

I gazed frantically around the room. How could I get her attention? How could I make her see me?

A black umbrella tilted against the corner of the wall caught my eye. If I could climb up the umbrella onto the handle, I'd be tall enough for Carla to see me.

I stepped up to the umbrella. It rose up like a tree above me. It wouldn't be an easy climb. But I was so close…so close to a cure…I couldn't give up now.

I grabbed the black fabric with both hands and started to pull myself up. My hands were moist and the umbrella fabric was slick and slippery.

I hoisted myself slowly, wrapping my legs around the long wires beneath the fabric. My hands kept sliding off. I kept slipping back down.

Halfway up I lost my hold and started to fall. My legs closed tightly around the umbrella. I held on...held on with my legs. Then slowly, panting, sweating, I pulled myself back up.

When I reached the metal point at the end of the black cloth, I had to stop and rest. Then I stretched out my hand and rubbed my fingers along the shiny wood handle. Testing it.

It felt very slippery, too. But I knew if I could pull myself up to its top, Carla would definitely be able to see me. Or at least hear me.

I kicked off from the umbrella point and began to shimmy up the fat, brown handle.

Almost there...almost there...

And then, there I was, breathless and weary— but standing on the umbrella handle. Standing tall and high enough for anyone to see me.

I did it! I *did* it !

My chest heaving, my heart pounding, I turned to the desk. And started to call to Carla.

I saw that she was gone.

CHAPTER 19

Her desk chair was pulled out and empty.

I let out a cry—and started to lose my balance. I lurched forward and nearly fell off the umbrella.

And then I heard a scream. A shrill scream of fright.

I spun around and saw Carla in front of me, hands pressed against her cheeks, face bright red, mouth open in another high scream.

The door to the examining room swung open, and Dr. Hayward, stethoscope swinging from side to side in front of him, came bursting in. "Carla—what on earth is wrong?"

Carla didn't answer. She just pointed, pointed at me with a trembling hand.

Dr. Hayward placed a calming hand on the shoulder of her white uniform. "It's okay," he said softly.

He bent over and brought his face close to mine, so close I could smell the minty mouthwash on his breath. "Danny?" he whispered. "Danny? You've shrunk so much?"

I nodded sadly. "I—I got here as fast as I could. Mom and Dad—"

"Your parents are frantic," he interrupted. "They've been searching everywhere for you. They're both out of their minds with worry."

"I fell out of the cage," I told him. "I hurried here. But it was so hard, I—"

"I'd better call them," Dr. Hayward said. He grabbed the phone receiver off Carla's desk. She stood in the center of the waiting room, arms crossed in front of her, staring at me in disbelief.

"Dr. Hayward—" I called. "Do you have a cure for me? Can you cure me right away?"

He didn't answer. He held the phone pressed tightly against his ear and listened. "They don't seem to be home, Danny. Maybe they are—"

The office door swung open. Mom and Dad burst in breathlessly. Mom's hair was wild. Her face was as pale as cake flour. Dad's shirt had come untucked from his pants. His eyes were red and bulging.

Dad spotted me first. "Danny? You're here?"

Mom sighed. "I don't believe it! You're here? You're okay?"

She rushed forward and picked me up. She set me down in the palm of her hand and stroked my back with one finger the way she used to pet my hamster.

"Danny, poor Danny," she whispered. A large teardrop fell from her face and splashed beside me on her palm.

"We're so sorry," Dad said, shaking his head. "When we saw that the cage was empty, we...we... didn't know what to do."

"It's okay," I told him. "We're here now. Let's get started with the cure. I don't really like sitting in Mom's hand."

We followed Dr. Hayward into his office. He stepped behind his big desk and motioned for us to sit down across from him. But my parents said they'd rather stand.

I sat cross-legged in Mom's palm. My heart was pounding. I couldn't bear the suspense. "So what is the cure?" I asked Dr. Hayward. "What do I have to do to get big again?"

Dr. Hayward let out a long sigh. His shoulders slumped. He shook his head. "I'm sorry, Danny. I called you all here because I thought I should give you the bad news in person. There is no cure."

CHAPTER 20

Dad carried me out of the doctor's office. Mom was sobbing too hard to hold me. Dad didn't say a word. He had bitten his bottom lip until it bled.

I was smaller than a mouse now. I was about the size of one of those tiny candy bars they make for Halloween.

At first when I heard the bad news, I felt like crying. But I guess I was too stunned to cry.

Riding in Dad's palm, I blinked against the blinding sunlight. We crossed the parking lot and stopped beside the car.

The light was so bright, I had to shut my eyes.

And as I covered them with both hands, an idea flashed into my mind.

A crazy idea. A crazy, *insane* idea.

But maybe that's the kind of idea we needed right now.

"Dad—!" I shouted up to him. "Dad—listen!"

He raised me close to his face. And now I could see that he had been crying, too. "What is it, Danny?" he choked out.

"Dad, I have a wild idea. Something that might make me big again. Or at least stop me from shrinking."

"Let's get out of this sun," Mom groaned.

We climbed into the front seat of the car. Dad turned the key and started the air conditioner. The cold air felt good against my burning skin.

Dad sat me down on top of the steering wheel. I was so short, my legs barely dangled over the side. "Danny, what's your idea?"

"Well…" I took a deep breath. "The bright sunlight reminded me of your movie projector."

Dad's eyes narrowed. "Huh? My projector?"

I nodded. "I just remembered something that happened. Megan and I went to see the Shrinkman movie. Then we came upstairs to visit you in the projection booth."

"Yes, yes. I remember," Dad said impatiently.

"Well, you were showing the Shrinkman movie, and I accidentally stepped in front of the projector. Remember?"

Dad nodded. "Go on."

"Danny, why are you telling us this?" Mom asked tearfully.

"Well...the light from the projector washed over me," I continued excitedly. "And it made me feel really funny. It just gave me a strange feeling. I felt sort of dazed. And then, right after that, I started to shrink."

Dad scratched his hair. "I don't understand. What are you trying to say?"

"Maybe...just maybe..." I started, "maybe the light did something to me. You know. Changed my molecules or something. And maybe, if I stand in front of the projector again, it will reverse the process, and I'll start to grow again."

Mom sighed and buried her face in her hands.

"But the theater isn't showing the Shrinkman movie anymore," Dad said, frowning, still biting his cut lip.

"What are you showing?" I asked.

He thought for a moment. *"Attack of the Fifty-Foot Woman."*

"That's perfect!" I cried. "Awesome!" I pressed my hands together in a begging position. "We have to try it, Dad. We have to!"

The five o'clock show had just begun. Only ten or twelve people were in the theater watching it.

Dad carried me up the steep steps to the projection room. Mom followed silently behind. She hadn't said a word since Dad had agreed to try my idea.

Ernie Rawls, a big, jolly-looking red-faced man, had taken Dad's place for the day. Dad waved to him and asked how it was going.

"Pretty quiet," Ernie replied.

Dad leaned close to Ernie and talked in a low whisper. I couldn't hear him, but I guessed that he was telling Ernie what we planned to do.

The projector whirred behind us, shooting its beam of light down to the screen. I peeked out another hole to the theater and saw the Fifty-Foot Woman rampaging around on the screen.

Dad raised me close to his face. "Okay, let's try it," he whispered. "I'm going to hold you in the projector light, Danny."

"Just for a few seconds, Dad," I instructed. "I was only in it for a second or two the first time."

Dad nodded.

I turned to see how Mom was doing, but she leaned against the back wall, her face hidden in darkness.

"It's going to work, Dad," I said as he stepped to the side of the big projector. "I know it's going to work!"

"Here goes," Dad said.

He raised his arm slowly. Held me in front of the beam of light.

And once again, the white light shot over me, blinded me, held me…dazed me.

CHAPTER 21

I blinked hard, shaking my head, trying to clear it as Dad lowered me from the light beam. He set me down on the worktable. He and Mom and Ernie leaned close, staring down at me. Waiting...

Watching...

Nothing happened.

The bright light faded from my eyes. The dazed feeling faded, too. I stared at my arms, my legs, watching for any sign that they were starting to grow.

No.

"Maybe it takes time," Dad said.

Mom had her hands pressed against the sides of her face. "The last time you didn't start to change right away?" She said it as a question.

"Yeah," I replied glumly. "It took a little while." But I knew this idea was a failure. I didn't feel any different. I knew I wasn't going to grow.

I'm doomed, I thought, starting to tremble. I hugged myself tightly to stop the shaking. I'm doomed...

The hours passed slowly. By night I still hadn't changed.

Mom and Dad kept me in the birdcage on the kitchen table. Mom gave me a few tiny shreds of tuna fish between some white bread crumbs for dinner. I drank orange juice from the thimble, but it was starting to get too heavy for me to pick up.

Dad had been on the phone all afternoon, calling doctors all around the country. He hoped to find a doctor who had some kind of idea about how to stop me from shrinking to nothing.

About an hour after dinner Mom and Dad came into the kitchen and leaned close to talk to me. I could see they were dressed to go out.

"We found a specialist at the hospital across town who has an idea," Mom said.

"He wants to talk to us before he sees you," Dad added. "We'll be back in an hour, maybe less."

"Will you be okay?" Mom asked.

I sat on the cage floor with my chin in my hands. "Yeah. Sure," I muttered.

"Don't give up hope," Mom said. Her voice broke as she said it. They threw me kisses and disappeared out the kitchen door. I heard the car start, then heard it back down the driveway.

I climbed to my feet and started to pace back and forth. I was so short now, I couldn't reach the perch swing above my head.

"I'm going to disappear forever," I whispered.

A sound from the living room made me stop. I stood in the center of the cage and listened.

I heard the front door swing open. Heard the hushed scrape of footsteps in the hall.

Someone trying not to be heard.

"Who's there?" I called. My voice was so tiny, I knew it didn't reach beyond the cage.

"Who's there?" I squeaked again.

More soft footsteps. A muffled cough.

Who had sneaked into my house? A thief?

A chill ran down my back. I ran to the cage bars and peered out.

A figure moved quickly into the kitchen.

"Megan—!" I cried. "Megan—I'm so glad it's you!"

I don't think she heard me. Her eyes searched the kitchen until she found the birdcage. Then she hurried across the room and picked up the cage.

The cage swung wildly, knocking me to the floor. "Hey—careful!" I shouted.

"Take it easy, Danny," she called in. "I'm late." Holding the cage high in front of her, she began trotting to the front door.

"Late?" I squeaked. "What do you mean late? Stop, Megan! Where are you taking me?"

She carried me outside and slammed the door behind her. It was a cool, breezy evening. A gust of wind blew me against the cage bars.

"Megan—stop!" I pleaded. "Put me back! I have to stay home! Why are you doing this?"

My cage swung wildly as she trotted to the driveway.

"Tonight is the Science Fair," she called down to me. "I need you there."

"Huh? Need me? Why?"

She stopped and raised me close to her face. Her dark eyes flashed excitedly. "Don't you get it, Danny? You're my science project!"

CHAPTER 22

I let out a shocked cry. The cage started to bounce and swing again as Megan took off, jogging toward school.

"Me?" I cried. "I'm your project? I—I don't get it, Megan!"

"You're my science project," she repeated, not slowing down as she ran across the street. "I told you, I *have* to win the prize. I really want that thousand dollars."

"But—but—" I sputtered. "You mean *you* made me shrink?"

"Of course," she replied calmly.

"How?" I demanded.

"In the science lab. That glass of liquid you drank when you choked on your chewing gum. You thought it was water. But it was my secret formula."

I was shaking so hard, I could barely speak. I felt shocked and angry and terrified all at the same time. "S-secret formula?"

"My great-grandmother Hester wrote the recipe in her journal. And she passed her journal on to me. I told you about Granny Hester. She lived about a hundred years ago. I told you she was a witch."

I sank to the cage floor, suddenly feeling too weak to stand. "I can't believe you did this to me, Megan. I thought you were my friend."

Baker Elementary School came into view on the next block. All the lights were on because of the Science Fair. "Of course, I'm your friend, Danny," Megan said, starting to jog faster.

"But you let me shrink and shrink!" I cried. "You knew what was happening the whole time."

"I have to win the money," she said flatly.

I grabbed the cage bars and stared out at her. "But what happens to me *after* the fair?" I shouted.

In the dim evening light I saw a strange smile spread over Megan's face. "I'll take care of you," she whispered.

CHAPTER 23

"And what is your project, Tim?"

Mr. Clarkus and the other three judges stood across the table from me. They had been moving from table to table in the school gym, examining each project, questioning the kids about them.

Now they stared down at the glass cage Tim Parsons had set up. "Is that a guinea pig or a white rat?" Mr. Clarkus asked.

"Why are they wasting time with Tim?" Megan whispered, standing behind my cage. "Why don't they just come over here and give me the prize?"

"It's a white rat," Tim told the teacher. "My study is about what is a good diet for white rats. I fed one rat only vegetables and the other rat only cereal."

The judges stared into the glass cage. "But, Tim, I see only one rat here," a judge said.

"I know. The other one died," Tim said. "So I couldn't really finish the experiment."

From my cage across the table, I watched Tim lift the white rat from its cage. "This is the one that ate cereal," he said.

It's twice my size, I thought sadly. I don't believe this. I'm smaller than a white rat. I shook my head and shut my eyes. I opened them when I heard a startled scream.

And saw the white rat leap from Tim's hands.

"Get him!" Mr. Clarkus shouted.

Tim made a wild grab—and missed.

Other hands grabbed at the rat. But it was too fast for them. Its pink feet slipped and slid as it scrabbled furiously across the table.

"No—" I uttered a cry as it darted straight to my cage.

It rose up in front of me. Its pink nose twitched. Its black eyes rolled as it saw me. It opened its mouth wide, revealing two rows of pointed teeth.

"Please—grab it! Take it away!" I shrieked.

The white rat hissed at me. And to my horror it grabbed the door between its pointed teeth and jerked it open.

"Nooooooo!" I wailed in horror as the rat leaped into the cage. I backed away. Backed away. Waving my hands wildly, trying to scare it.

But I must have looked like a tasty little food morsel to the hulking creature. It opened its mouth, and pearly drool slid over its teeth. "Help me! Somebody! Megan!" I shrieked.

The giant rat backed me against the bars. Then it rose up on its hind legs, hissing, drooling hungrily, eyes rolling in its huge head.

A T-Rex vision flashed into my panicked mind. The rat stood over me like a dinosaur!

And then lunged for my throat.

I shut my eyes again.

I waited for the crushing pain. Waited to feel my skin ripped off in the creature's pointed teeth.

But…no.

I opened my eyes to see Megan dangling the rat by the tail. She held it over the table and returned it to Tim.

"Saved your life, Danny," she whispered to me.

Trembling, I opened my mouth to reply, but no sound came out.

I suddenly realized the judges were no longer across the table. All four of them had bent down to stare into the cage at me. Their startled cries echoed off the cage bars.

"What on earth—?" Mr. Clarkus gasped.

"Megan—what is that? *Who* is that?"

"This can't be your experiment—can it?"

"It looks just like Danny Marin!" Mr. Clarkus declared. "A tiny Danny Marin."

"It *is* Danny Marin!" Megan proclaimed proudly. "I used a special formula to shrink him."

Mr. Clarkus let out a scream. The judges all uttered shocked cries.

"Unbelievable! Call the newspaper—immediately!"

"This is astounding! Megan, you'll be famous!"

"Call the TV stations! No one will believe this!"

"You'll be famous! Famous!"

Mr. Clarkus handed Megan the check for a thousand dollars.

The entire gym went into a frenzy. Shouts and cheers. A hundred kids came crushing around the table, eager to see Megan's miracle freak.

The noise was deafening to me. The faces, the staring faces were making me dizzy and sick. I sat down on the cage floor, rested my back against a bar, and buried my face in my hands.

For the first time I felt more angry than frightened. In fact, I felt so angry I was about to burst.

It was insane. The shouts and startled cries. The amazed faces. The newspaper photographers. The TV interviewers.

It seemed to go on for hours. The whole while, Megan's smile never faded. It was her night of victory, her big triumph.

Tiny Danny was famous, too. Tiny Danny, the shrinking boy.

My ears still buzzed, my head felt heavy as lead when everyone finally left. The lights in the gym dimmed. The crew of custodians began to clean up.

"Megan—I have to go home," I called hoarsely. "Take me home now—and then I never want to see your face again."

She picked up the cage. Her eyes flashed in the dim light. "Don't say that, Danny. Or I won't cure you."

"Huh? Cure?" My heart started to race.

"Of course I'm going to cure you," she said, carrying the cage against her chest. She stepped out of the gym, into the long front hall. "I'm your friend, Danny. I wouldn't let you disappear."

"But—h-how—?" I whispered.

"I mixed a bottle of my Great-grandma Hester's *growing* potion," she said, turning into the science lab. She clicked on the overhead lights. "Granny Hester made you small. And now she'll make you normal-sized again."

I let out a long sigh of relief. "You're really going to cure me?"

"Of course. Right away." She set the cage down on a table and disappeared into the supply closet.

A few seconds later she appeared carrying a glass beaker. As she came closer, I saw that the beaker contained a clear liquid.

"This is the growth formula," Megan said. She picked up a bowl and poured the liquid from the beaker into the bowl.

"I'm going to hold you over the side of the bowl so you can drink from it," she explained. "Drink as much as you can, Danny. You'll be back to normal size in a few hours. I promise."

"Oh, thank you!" I cried happily. I had forgotten my anger. I couldn't think about that now. I could only think of being a normal-sized guy again.

"Hurry," I said. "I can't stand being this small for one second longer."

Megan carried the bowl in two hands. Balancing it carefully, she took two steps toward my cage.

And tripped over the leg of a lab stool.

The bowl flew out of her hands and clattered into a sink.

And I stared in horror as the thick, clear liquid poured down the drain.

CHAPTER 24

"Ohhhhhhh noooooo." I sank to my knees on the cage floor.

My stomach lurched. I felt sick.

Megan gazed at the empty bowl in the sink. "I...don't...believe...this..." she murmured.

But then her expression changed. "Look, Danny. There's a little left at the bottom of the beaker." She held up the glass beaker. "It should be enough. You're so tiny now, you couldn't drink much anyway. You're no bigger than a beetle."

"H-hurry," I said in a whisper. "Please."

She found an eyedropper. I watched her tilt the beaker and squeeze the tiny bit of liquid into it. She started to carry the eyedropper to the cage.

"Careful!" I warned. "Watch out for the stool."

She stepped around it. She leaned over the cage and lowered the eyedropper to my mouth.

I didn't hesitate. I pressed my lips against the tip and drank. Drank thirstily, sucking down the cold, clear liquid.

"According to Granny Hester's journal, you'll start to grow instantly," Megan said.

Tilting my head under the eyedropper, I drank a little more. Then I stepped back, licking my lips.

"Feel anything?" Megan asked.

I took a deep breath. "Not yet."

"It should be any second," she said.

We waited.

Seconds went by. A minute. Two minutes. Three.

I didn't grow. I didn't feel any different.

Ten minutes later Megan and I were still staring at each other.

Nothing happened.

She sank onto the lab stool with a sigh. "Failure," she whispered. "The growth formula is a failure." She shook her head sadly. "Danny, do you know what that means?"

"That I'm going to disappear forever?"

"No." She frowned, shaking her head. "It means that my *shrinking* formula didn't work, either. I always followed Granny Hester's recipes perfectly. But they don't work. I'm not the one who shrunk you, Danny. I'm a fraud. I'm a failure. When all those TV and newspaper reporters find out, I'll be a national disgrace."

"But, Megan—" I started. "Maybe—"

"Be quiet a minute, Danny. Let me think. This is horrible!"

I wasn't in the mood to feel sorry for Megan. I knew I had only an hour or so left.

"Are you sure your formula didn't shrink me?"

She sighed again. "Yes, I'm sure. I'm a total fraud."

"Then something else did it…" I said, thinking out loud.

And suddenly it came to me. The Shrinkman Cola. That awful drink I had at the movie theater.

If it wasn't Megan's potion, it had to be the Shrinkman Cola. Or maybe...the combination. First I drank Megan's shrinking formula. Then I had the Shrinkman drink. Then I stepped into the light.

Yes! Maybe all three things *together* made me shrink.

It was a wild idea. Maybe it was totally crazy, totally wrong. But I had no choice.

"Megan—hurry," I said. "You have to take me to the movie theater!"

We ran into the lobby. It was after ten o'clock, and the last shows of the day were running. The lobby was empty. The lights had been dimmed. A tall, dark-haired girl in a red-and-white striped uniform was sponging off the popcorn counter.

Carrying my cage in front of her, Megan ran across the lobby, to the back corner where we had found the Shrinkman Cola vending machine.

We both cried out at the same time.

Gone! The vending machine was gone!

"This can't be happening," Megan murmured. She whirled around. The cage flew wildly from side to side as Megan ran to the popcorn stand.

"The drink machine—" she called breathlessly. "Where is it? Where?"

The girl behind the counter stopped sponging. She squinted at Megan. "The drink machine? Which one?"

Megan pointed frantically to the corner of the lobby. "The Shrinkman drink machine. Where is it? We need a bottle!"

The girl made a face. "That disgusting stuff? It was gross. Everyone was complaining about it. So we sent that vending machine back."

CHAPTER 25

I wanted to scream, but I felt too weak.

I was no bigger than a bug. In an hour or so I'd be as tiny as a flea.

And then I'd be gone.

"That truck driver was so late," the girl told Megan. "Would you believe he didn't show up till ten to take that drink machine? I think he's still in the parking lot around back."

That's all Megan had to hear. She took off, my cage swinging crazily at her side.

"Hey—where's your bird?" I heard the popcorn girl call.

But Megan didn't stop. She raced out the front door of the theater, then along the narrow walk that led to the parking lot in back.

The blue-uniformed driver was still hoisting the drink machine onto the back of his truck. Megan begged him for one bottle of Shrinkman Cola. He argued with her. He said he was too late.

Megan pulled a ten-dollar bill from her pocket and handed it to him. The man shoved it quickly into his uniform pants pocket. He opened the back of the machine and handed Megan a bottle.

"I don't know how anyone can drink this stuff," he said.

Megan didn't reply. Carrying the birdcage in one hand and the bottle in the other, she ran back to the side of the theater.

No one in sight. I could hear the music from the movie inside the theater.

Megan set my cage down on the pavement. She twisted open the bottle of Shrinkman Cola. She lowered the bottle to the cage bars. But I was too tiny to drink from it.

"Here, Danny." She poured a puddle of the brown drink onto the cage floor. "Hurry."

I dropped to my hands and knees and lowered my face to the puddle. I lapped it up, drinking like a dog.

It tasted awful. But I didn't care.

Would it work?

I felt a sharp tingling in my chest. The feeling spread to my arms and legs.

I felt myself start to stretch.

"Megan—better lift me out of the cage," I called.

She pulled me out just in time. My head, my chest, my arms, my legs—all were stretching, growing...

Yes! *Yes!*

It took less than a minute.

I stood there laughing, cheering, gleeful tears running down my face. Stood there in my shredded pajamas. Normal size. Normal again.

Danny Marin, Normal Guy.

I was so happy, I hugged Megan.

Can you imagine the greeting I got from my parents?

First they were stunned. Then they laughed. Then they hugged me. Then they cried.

Then we all cried. We were so happy.

The next morning they didn't want me to go to school. They wanted to take me to Dr. Hayward.

But I had to go to school. Today was the big game, our long-awaited basketball game against Stern Valley.

I was the star of the team. I had to be there.

Just before the game, Megan met me outside the gym. Through the gym doors I could hear kids cheering and shouting. Both teams were already warming up on the court.

"Are you okay?" Megan asked. "Do you feel all right, Danny?"

Before I could reply, I felt that sharp tingling in my chest again. Once again the tingling spread rapidly through my body.

"Something is happening," I told Megan.

And then I shot up. Growing more. Growing until my head hit the ceiling.

"Danny—" Megan gasped. "The ceiling is nine feet tall. Oh no! No! You're nine feet tall!"

I swallowed hard. "I don't believe this."

"Wait. I still have the shrink formula in the science lab," Megan said. "And I kept the rest of the Shrinkman Cola. Come with me, Danny. Hurry. I'll get you back to normal size in no time."

I started to follow her. I had to bend my head to keep it from scraping the ceiling.

I took two or three loping steps. Then stopped.

I listened to the cheers in the gym.

It's time for the biggest basketball game of the year, I thought.

And I'm nine feet tall!

I spun away from Megan. "Danny—where are you going?" she called. "Danny—?"

I bent down and pushed open the gym doors with my mile-long arms. "Hey, guys—" I shouted. "Guys! I'm ready to play!"

ABOUT THE AUTHOR

Photograph © Dan Nelken

R.L. (Robert Lawrence) Stine is one of the best-selling children's authors in history. His Goosebumps series, along with such series as Fear Street, The Nightmare Room, Rotten School, and Mostly Ghostly have sold nearly 400 million books in this country alone. And they are translated into 32 languages.

The *Goosebumps* TV series was the top-rated kids' series for three years in a row. R.L.'s TV movies, including *The Haunting Hour: Don't Think About It* and *Mostly Ghostly*, are perennial Halloween favorites. And his scary TV series, *R.L. Stine's The Haunting Hour*, is in its second season on The Hub network.

R.L. continues to turn out Goosebumps books, published by Scholastic. In addition, his first horror novel for adults in many years, titled *Red Rain*, will be published by Touchstone books in October 2012.

R.L. says that he enjoys his job of "scaring kids." But the biggest thrill for him is turning kids on to reading.

R.L. lives in New York City with his wife, Jane, an editor and publisher, and King Charles Spaniel, Minnie. His son, Matthew, is a sound designer and music producer.

R.L. STINE'S

THE
HAUNTING
HOUR
THE SERIES.

Don't Let Your Parents Watch it Alone!

Only on The Hub TV Channel!
Visit hubworld.com
for channel listings and showtimes.